Written by JUDY COX

Illustrated by EMILY ARNOLD McCULLY

Rabbit Pirates

A TALE OF THE SPINACH MAIN

 Browndeer Press Harcourt Brace & Company *San Diego New York London*

Glossary

au contraire—on the contrary

aubergines—eggplants

bon—good

coup de grâce—finishing stroke

cuisine—food

le déjeuner—lunch

l'eau—water

minuit—midnight

mon ami—my friend

mon vieux—my old friend

monsieur—Mister

non—no

tête-à-tête—private conversation

très—very

très bonne—very good

vin ordinaire—table wine

The illustrations in this book were done in watercolor on 140 lb. Arches paper.
The display type and cartouche were created by Georgia Deaver.
The text type was set in Granjon.
Color separations by United Graphic Pte. Ltd., Singapore
Printed and bound by Tien Wah Press, Singapore
This book was printed on totally chlorine-free Nymolla Matte Art paper.
Production supervision by Stanley Redfern and Pascha Gerlinger
Designed by Lori McThomas Buley

Browndeer Press is a registered trademark of Harcourt Brace & Company.

Library of Congress Cataloging-in-Publication Data
Cox, Judy.
Rabbit pirates: a tale of the Spinach Main/Judy Cox; illustrated by Emily Arnold McCully.
p.   cm.
"Browndeer Press."
Summary: Two old rabbit friends disagree about many things, including when and how to deal with the tricky fox who threatens to ruin the business at their restaurant in the Provence region of France.
ISBN 0-15-201832-8
[1. Rabbits—Fiction. 2. Foxes—Fiction. 3. Restaurants—Fiction. 4. Friendship—Fiction.] I. McCully, Emily Arnold, ill. II. Title.
PZ7.C83835Rab   1999
[E]—dc21   98-17481

First edition
F E D C B A

Printed in Singapore

For my family and friends
—J. C.

To Jerry and Paula
—E. A. M.

In sunny Provence there can be found a small café known as the Spinach Main. The Spinach Main is famous for its fresh salads and crusty homemade bread.

The host of the Spinach Main is Monsieur Lapin. He is most unusual. His friend, the chef, Monsieur Blanc, is *très* strange as well. There is something nautical about the pair. Perhaps they are really pirates? Who knows? They will not say.

Monsieur Lapin and Monsieur Blanc serve the best salads in Provence at the Spinach Main. There are vegetables sautéed in garlic butter and thinly sliced onions, radishes and asparagus, green beans that crunch when bitten, vine-ripened tomatoes, and tender fresh lettuces that Monsieur Blanc grows in his garden.

Word of the excellent cuisine at the Spinach Main has spread throughout Provence. Business is good.

But perhaps some of those who hear of the restaurant have things in mind other than tender lettuces and vine-ripened tomatoes.

On slow, hot afternoons, Monsieur Lapin and Monsieur
Blanc take their glasses of mineral water out to the terrace and
sit together, side by side, reminiscing in the sun. "Life is
peaceful, eh, *mon ami*?" says Monsieur Lapin.

"Not like the old days, my friend," agrees Monsieur Blanc.
"Remember our first meeting?"

"How could I forget? The battle at Tortuga, was it not? The
cannons' roar! The clash of swords! It was there that you had
the good fortune to be rescued by me." Monsieur Lapin's eyes
shine at the memory.

"*You* rescued *me*? *Au contraire!*" exclaims Monsieur Blanc. "It was *I* who rescued *you*! We were attacked by buccaneers. You were pinned to the ship's rail. I grabbed the rope over-head. With great courage, I swung across the deck and kicked the villains out of the way!"

"Not at all, *mon ami*." Monsieur Lapin shakes his head. "Were it not for the excellence of my fencing, you would now be bait for the sharks."

"It was my courage!" declares Monsieur Blanc, leaping to his feet.

"My sword!"

"Courage!" Monsieur Blanc glares at his friend, looking for all the world as if he would fight him now.

But Monsieur Lapin merely laughs and passes a dish of shallots. "Ah, well. Perhaps my memory is not so good as it was," he says mildly.

Monsieur Blanc sits back down. He shrugs. "You may be right. Perhaps I forget." He nibbles a shallot and puts his feet up. "In any case, life is *très bonne* now."

One day, as Monsieur Blanc and Monsieur Lapin are in the
kitchen preparing *aubergines* for the lunch they will serve that
day, a well-dressed fox comes into the dining room of the café.
Sunlight glints off his sharp teeth as he seats himself at a table
and picks up the menu.

"That Reynard, he is a bad one, *non?*" murmurs Monsieur
Lapin to Monsieur Blanc as they peer into the dining room
from behind the swinging door.

"Shall we fight him?" asks Monsieur Blanc, his pink eyes shining at the idea.

"No, indeed," says Monsieur Lapin with dignity. "We will see what Monsieur Reynard will have for *le déjeuner*." And he waits on the fox.

The fox orders, and Monsieur Lapin and Monsieur Blanc serve him bread and salad and a glass of *vin ordinaire*. When Monsieur Reynard is finished, he kisses his fingertips. "My compliments to the chef!" he says with a bow. "I look forward to eating you—I mean, eating *here* again, soon."

That evening Monsieur Blanc is in his garden harvesting his cabbages. He is thinking about the soup he will make. He does not see the fox slinking through the radishes. The fox crouches to spring—Monsieur Blanc bends lower to pull up a cabbage . . . and . . .

Something is not right!

Monsieur Blanc catches sight of the fox and takes aim.
He hurls his cabbage. It flies through the air like a cannonball
and strikes Reynard on his tender snout.

"Round one to you, monsieur," the fox mutters, holding his
paw over his wounded nose. "But what about round two?"
And he disappears into the dusk.

Monsieur Lapin comes out on the terrace to see what all the fuss is about.

"Now do we fight?" demands Monsieur Blanc. "That fox, he will be back."

Monsieur Lapin pats him on the arm. "No, *mon ami*. We wait and see what we shall see."

The next day Monsieur Reynard again chooses to dine at the Spinach Main. This time the restaurant is filled with guests. The Mouse sisters are there with their aunt. The Goose family enjoys a meal at the corner table. Madame and Monsieur Canard are having a *tête-à-tête* at a table for two.

Conversation stops when Monsieur Reynard enters. He slowly looks around the room. He licks his chops. One by one the other guests hurriedly finish their meals and leave. Soon the Spinach Main is empty.

"This is a fine place you have here. Such tasty patrons! I mean, *portions*! I hope to eat here often," comments Monsieur Reynard, when Monsieur Lapin comes to take his order. His yellow eyes gleam. "I find you—and your restaurant, of course—simply irresistible."

When he finishes his meal, Monsieur Reynard leaves a big tip and saunters out.

Monsieur Blanc fingers the money. "What an insult! Does he think we are waiters?" He scornfully tosses the money back onto the table. "Do we fight now?" he asks with a longing glance at the cutlasses and pistols above the mantel.

"No," says Monsieur Lapin. "We are men of peace now. We do not fight."

Monsieur Blanc looks around at the empty tables. "But that fox! He will ruin our business!"

Monsieur Lapin does not answer. But he fears his friend is right.

At dawn Monsieur Lapin, Monsieur Blanc, and their friend Monsieur Cochon roam the woods hunting for truffles. Monsieur Cochon wanders across the meadow. Monsieur Lapin digs under a large tree. Monsieur Blanc digs behind the ferns. He does not see his friend step into a rope snare. *Whoosh!* Monsieur Lapin is whisked upward and dangles, upside down, in the air.

"Quickly, *mon ami*!" Monsieur Lapin calls. "All hands aloft!"

Monsieur Blanc swarms up the tree. With his truffle knife he saws the rope in half. Monsieur Lapin tumbles into the soft ferns.

Rustle, rustle. Someone is coming. Monsieur Blanc drops down. He and Monsieur Lapin hide themselves in the bushes.

It is Monsieur Reynard. He picks up the cut rope. "They have escaped again," he murmurs. "But next time! Ah, next time will be different." He pads away into the shadows.

"Now!" whispers Monsieur Lapin. He leaps up, brandishing a stick. "Now we fight!"

Monsieur Blanc pulls him back. "*Non, mon vieux,*" he whispers. "Not now, my old friend."

"But that Reynard! He will stop at nothing!"

Monsieur Blanc smiles. His whiskers curl up. "I have a plan."

They close the restaurant and work all day. "So rabbits are irresistible to Monsieur Reynard," laughs Monsieur Blanc as they work. "We shall see about that!"

The stars glow softly in the warm summer night. The church bell rings twelve times. *Minuit.* The Spinach Main is dark and quiet. Monsieur Reynard creeps toward the café, slinking through the bushes, as dark as a shadow. Only his sharp teeth gleam like daggers, and the white tip of his tail glows in the moonlight.

On soft paws, he pads across the terrace. Dark shapes catch his eye. "Hmm," he murmurs. "The rabbits sit up late to admire the moon. For me, a midnight snack!"

Closer, closer, he steals. He crouches. Suddenly he springs to the chair. He grabs a rabbit. He takes a huge bite.

"AUGH!" he cries. "Water! *L'eau!*" He flees, his tail dragging, his tongue hanging out, his eyes wild. He dashes down the hillside, crashing through the bushes, never to be seen again.

The next day Monsieur Lapin slices onions into neat rings for the thick onion soup he will make. Monsieur Blanc kneads dough for the bread.

"Our little pastry rabbits certainly set a fire under that fox!" says Monsieur Lapin.

"A fire *in* that fox you mean!" Monsieur Blanc agrees.

"It was my pastry that fooled him," says Monsieur Lapin. "The carrot whiskers were the *coup de grâce*." He waves his hand. "The finishing stroke!"

"*Au contraire,*" says Monsieur Blanc. "It was my garlic, onions, and hot peppers that set the fire."

"But it was my pastry that looked so much like you."

"Garlic and onions!"

"Pastry!" Monsieur Lapin glares, looking for all the world as if he would fight his friend this minute.

But Monsieur Blanc only shrugs. "Perhaps you are right, *mon ami*. Perhaps it was your pastry."

Monsieur Lapin laughs and continues slicing his onions. "*Non, non, mon ami*. I'm sure it was your peppers and garlic." He bites a radish picked that morning from the garden. It crunches. "*Bon!*" he exclaims, and kisses his fingers.

There is always a lot of work to be done in a café. And
when the work is done, Monsieur Lapin and Monsieur Blanc
will rest themselves on the terrace, glasses in hand, and watch
the sunset. Life is *très bonne* at the Spinach Main.

$16.00

DATE			